Dorothy KOOMSON

The Beach Wedding

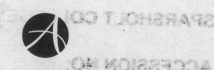
arrow books

1 3 5 7 9 10 8 6 4 2

Arrow Books
20 Vauxhall Bridge Road
London SW1V 2SA

Arrow Books is part of the Penguin Random House group of companies
whose addresses can be found at global.penguinrandomhouse.com.

Penguin
Random House
UK

First published in Great Britain by Arrow Books in 2018

www.penguin.co.uk

A CIP catalogue record for this book is available from the British Library.

ISBN 9781784756383
ISBN 9781473538382 (ebook)

Typeset in ITC Stone Serif 12/16 pt by Jouve (UK), Milton Keynes
Printed and bound in Great Britain by Clays Ltd, St Ives Plc

MIX
Paper from
responsible sources
FSC® C018179

Penguin Random House is committed to a
sustainable future for our business, our readers
and our planet. This book is made from Forest
Stewardship Council® certified paper.

The Beach Wedding

Dorothy Koomson, Totally Beached

Dorothy Koomson has been making up stories since she was thirteen and hasn't stopped since. She is the author of twelve novels including *The Friend, When I Was Invisible, The Chocolate Run,* and *The Ice Cream Girls.* While writing *The Beach Wedding,* Dorothy spent a lot of time thinking of all the wonderful beaches she's visited in her life.

For more info on Dorothy Koomson and her books, visit www.dorothykoomson.co.uk

To all readers out there.

1

24 years ago

'Don't, Drew, please don't!' I shouted as he ripped off his tie and jacket while running across the beach. We'd heard shouting, the cries of a mother whose little boy had been swept out to sea. And Drew, my fiancé, didn't think twice. He just ran towards the water.

'Wait for the lifeguards,' I called after him, but he didn't stop. He ran out as far as he could. He was just ahead of his best friend, Jake, and two of the staff members from Bussu Bay, the beach hotel where we were staying. He was different from the others, though – that was why I told him not to go. He wasn't as strong a swimmer. He wasn't at ease in the water. It wouldn't take too much for him to get into trouble out there. It wouldn't take too much for 'Don't, Drew, please don't!' to be the last words he ever heard me say.

Nia & Marvin

Invite you to their beach wedding!

On: **2 March 2018**

At: **Bussu Bay Beach Resort
(Ghana)**

11 am till you drop

Rooms, food, water sports, booze all included

(We don't really expect any of
you to come, so there'll be a party in
Brighton when we get home.)

(But do come if you can – Bussu
Bay totally rocks!)

3

Now

'Mum, this is Marvin. Marvin, this is my mum, Tessa. You can call her Ms Dannall.'

It's still hard for me to believe that I have a daughter who is old enough to drive a car, drink alcohol, vote – and get married. Which is what my little girl will be doing at our family beach resort in just under a week.

They've just arrived from Brighton and they both look jet-lagged, but happy and excited to be here.

I stare very hard at Marvin, my daughter's fiancé. This is the first time I have met him in real life. He is often there when I video-call Nia, and he seems polite and nice. But he wants to marry my daughter, so he has to be more than polite and nice – he needs to be amazing. They met doing work experience at an IT company two years ago and have been together ever since.

I'm not sure what I make of you yet, I think to myself.

'I am not sure what I make of you yet,' my 70-year-old mother actually says. 'I am not sure if you are good enough for my precious granddaughter.'

Bussu Bay Beach Resort is our family home and business in Ghana, West Africa. My parents opened it nearly thirty years ago – and ran it until about four years ago when I had to take over. My mother, who was in charge of the resort while my father took care of the water-sports side of things, fell and broke her hip. Even with all the help and staff they had, they couldn't see how to keep the business going in the way they wanted so they talked about selling it. I was living in Brighton, England, I had a great job and a great life, but I couldn't let them sell this place when it had been all they had worked for. So I had to move here and take over.

It'd been such a difficult decision. I hated the thought of leaving Brighton, and I hated leaving Nia, but I especially hated the idea of living here after what had happened twenty-four years ago. But I had no choice – my parents needed me. Now that my mum doesn't have to worry about the business, she enjoys bossing me around. And she enjoys embarrassing her granddaughter.

'I suppose you are almost handsome,' my mother says to Marvin.

Nia glares at me, trying to tell me to control her grandmother. I want to laugh in my daughter's face and ask her: *since when have I ever been able to control my mother?*

'Mother,' I say and hook my arm through hers, 'let's go and show the happy couple where they'll be sleeping.'

I whisper to Nia and Marvin, 'It's the Honeymoon Suite.' Over the years, our resort has grown from ten rooms to fifty, all varying in size. For Nia and Marvin, I have chosen the biggest room that is part of the main complex, with views out over the large green palm trees and the ocean. As well as a luxury bath and shower, it has its own private patio where they can have breakfast in peace, and a little path leads down to the drop-off where the beach begins.

My mum stops and, leaning heavily on her walking stick, she turns to me. She looks at me like she is about to tell me off.

'Honeymoon?' she says sternly. 'Do you see a wedding ring on my granddaughter's finger?'

Me and my big mouth, I groan inside. 'No,' I say.

'Then they will *not* be sleeping in the same room, let alone the room for those who are *married*.' When she says the last part, my mum turns to glare at Jake, my other half.

Mum is still so put out that we're not married,

but live under her roof, that I have to keep a room free for him. Every night, if Mum is up when Jake goes to bed, he has to declare, 'Goodnight all, I'm just off to my bedroom'. Otherwise she gives him one of her world-famous stares. Jake doesn't complain. Just like he didn't complain when we packed up and moved here. Mum continues to stare at poor Jake.

'Mama,' Jake says to my mother, raising his hands in peace, 'every other day I ask your daughter to marry me, and every other day, she says no.'

Mum shakes her head. 'Excuses, excuses, excuses.'

Nia says to Marvin, 'I'm sure I told you how Grandma and me both think Mum and Jake should be married by now. They've been together nearly twenty years and she still won't marry him. That's just wrong, isn't it?'

I smile at my daughter. I am so getting her back for that. 'So, seeing as you agree with Grandma about people who aren't married not sharing rooms, I think it's best that you each get a room on either side of Grandma and Grandpa's room?'

My grin gets even wider as Nia's mouth drops open.

'Sounds great,' Marvin says.

My daughter doesn't move. 'I can't believe you've just done that to me,' she says.

'Well, babe, to be fair, you did start it by mentioning her not being married,' Marvin says. 'And I think we've all learnt a valuable lesson today, don't you?'

'What lesson is that?' Nia asks him.

'Don't annoy your mother.'

I grin at him. 'Oh I like you, Marvin,' I say. 'I like you very, very much.'

Nia takes her wedding dress, hidden in a large silver cover. Marvin picks up some of their bags, and they begin to follow my mother down the hallway towards their rooms.

Before Jake and I move to gather up the rest of the luggage, we stare at each other. We haven't talked about it since Nia said she wanted to get married here. We haven't talked about it, but how could either of us forget the way the last wedding we went to on the beach changed our lives for ever?

4

Now

When my parents opened Bussu Bay nearly thirty years ago, everyone said they were crazy. No one would think to come to West Africa to dive, surf, fish, jet-ski or simply relax on the beach for two weeks. But my parents had an idea they believed in. This place was their dream, so they kept going despite what everyone else said. All those years ago, there had only been one posh hotel in the area and that was a bit of a walk from the beach. It took a while – five years, in fact – but people began to notice Bussu Bay and tell their friends. And they told their friends, who told their friends, until it became a place where people come back to again and again.

All along the coastline there are now other hotels and resorts. My parents were the first but not the last. This week I've decided to keep the resort private for the wedding, so only Nia and Marvin and family and friends will stay here.

After Nia and Marvin have showered, we eat dinner on the large patio with a corrugated-iron roof, attached to the dining room. The three cooks have laid on a feast that would feed twenty people, not six, and we are all absolutely stuffed.

The night is a beautiful silky black, the kind you never truly get in England. The blackness slips itself around your senses and mingles with the taste of the delicious food, the feel of the heat on your skin, and the sound of the ocean hitting the shore. Either Kwame or Edward, the only members of staff who live here full-time, is playing highlife music somewhere and the air around us is alive with the upbeat party rhythm.

Both Nia and Marvin have shiny faces from the heat, and their eyes keep closing as though they are going to fall asleep right there at the table. I love sitting here with my daughter – we haven't spent time together since I sent her the money to come here for Christmas two years ago. Mum and Dad have gone to bed because they have an early start.

Sitting here, I don't look at the ocean. It is gorgeous, and at night, when there is no wind, the water is like a sheet of black glass, but I still don't look at it. I can't. I don't collapse every time I see the ocean now, but it doesn't take much to make me feel like I am reliving the worst day of my life.

As if he knows I am becoming upset, Jake covers my hand with his, and gives me a reassuring squeeze. Reminding me that he's there. He was there that awful day and he's been there ever since.

In five days my daughter is going to stand on the beach, surrounded by family and a few friends, and get married. Like I tried to do, all those years ago. Sometimes, it feels like it happened yesterday. I remember the hot sand under my bare feet, the weight of the bouquet in my hands, the feeling that I was the happiest, prettiest woman in the world. And then the nightmare began.

'I'm going to bed,' I say. It's too much. I can't sit here, wondering what happened to Drew on what was meant to be the most perfect day of our lives.

My daughter coughs into her hand while saying, 'Lightweight.'

'Carry on, Nia, if you want to end up sharing a room with Grandma,' I say to her. 'You know I can make that happen.'

Jake and Marvin both laugh before we do our goodnights.

'I'm so glad you're here,' I tell my daughter.

I mean it, too. Despite everything, it feels right that she's come here to get married.

24 years ago

The little white boy's mother had been hysterical until Jake handed him back to her. Jake was the strongest swimmer of the men who had gone into the water so he had got to the child first and he was the first to come out again. The two other men who had tried to rescue the boy came out, coughing, until they collapsed on the sand. All of them would have had to fight to keep on swimming once they got out to sea. The water hadn't looked that rough, but it was tricky out there – you would think it was calm, but the undertow of the waves could suddenly suck you down.

My uncle was a doctor and had run to his room to get his medical bag. He was now working on the little boy. Jake had dropped on to the ground, trying to breathe normally again.

I stood at the water's edge, waiting for Drew to appear. I couldn't see him. Out in the waves, in the tossing and turning of the sea, I couldn't see him anywhere.

'Where is he?' I asked Jake.

'I didn't see him out there,' Jake said between coughs. He kept looking at the boy, who was now surrounded by people. 'I saw the other two, I got the boy, but I didn't see Drew.'

I looked at Jake, and then at my dad who was standing a little way behind him. Drew hadn't even been out on the fishing boat with my dad since we arrived because he hadn't been that strong a swimmer. *Why did he run into the water like that?* I asked myself. *What did he think he was doing?*

'You men, get the boats!' my father shouted. He could see what was going to happen. How this day, my wedding day, was going to end. 'Kumi,' he said to a young boy who often came to Bussu Bay to earn money helping with chores, 'you run and get the police. I will give you five hundred cedis if you run, fast-fast.'

Kumi took off at a speed I had never seen him move at before – he was a little boy, small and wiry, who did not like to exert himself. Mum always joked that he was storing up his energy for the day when the Almighty might call on him. I watched the boy become a blur at the corner of my eye while I frantically searched the sea. 'Where is he, Jake?' I said again, quieter this time since I knew Jake had no answer.

The men pushed the boats out into the water

but the sea seemed to resist, rising up and creating huge waves to push them back.

'He'll be OK,' Jake said. He was on his feet now and standing beside me. 'They'll find him.'

I stopped looking out to sea and I looked at Jake instead.

I heard it in his voice, and I saw it on his face: they weren't going to find Drew. Jake knew it. Just like I did. They weren't going to find my husband-to-be, Drew.

5

Now

When Jake slips under the mosquito net into bed beside me some time later, I'm wide awake and staring up at the ceiling. The heat hasn't dropped tonight, not like it usually does, and the ceiling fan is turning round and round above us.

'Thought you'd be asleep by now,' he says.

'I can't sleep,' I reply.

'Are you . . . Are you still thinking about . . .' Jake stops speaking. We've both been thinking about it, but we haven't talked about it. I roll over on to my side and stare at the blank wall.

'Have you thought about anything else since Nia said she was getting married here?' I reply.

'No, I haven't,' Jake says. 'Of course I haven't.'

24 years ago

'Come on, Tessa, you have to come back in.' Jake spoke gently and carefully to me. Many people had tried to make me leave the beach by saying they would run to fetch me if there was any news. I'd said no to them because I had to stay where I was. If I stayed where I was, wearing the white dress, he would see it. He was lost in the darkness of the ocean and seeing me waiting for him would give him something to come back to.

'No, I'm not moving,' I told Jake. We were alone on the beach – the search had been called off hours before because no one could have survived so long out there, they said. But I knew different; I knew Drew was coming back.

'Please, Tessa. You've had no food, you've barely drunk any water. In this heat that's dangerous. And,' he leaned in close and lowered his voice, 'it's no good for the baby.'

'How did you know?' I asked, shocked.

'Since I came out of the sea, you've had your hand on your stomach as though you're protecting a child.'

'Drew has to come back,' I told Jake. 'He doesn't even know that he was going to be a dad. I was going to tell him on our wedding night as a present. It was what he wanted and he would've been so happy. And I can't do it without him. I just can't.'

'You can,' Jake replied. 'You're one of the

strongest women I know. And you won't be alone. I'll be with you every step of the way.'

'He needs to come back to me,' I sobbed. 'I just need him to come back to me.'

Jake put his arms around me, hushed and rocked me as I cried and cried for the father of my child who had left me.

Now

'I'm sorry,' Jake says to me. We are so many years away from that day, but every so often, when he guesses I am thinking about Drew, Jake will say that. He will say sorry.

'It's not your fault,' I reply.

He still feels guilty that he came back and Drew didn't; and I feel guilty because, despite all the time that has passed, I still blame him for being alive and well when Drew was not.

24 years ago

Jake held the door open to my Brighton flat as I walked down the stairs.

It was two months after the wedding and I had only just managed to get home to Brighton from Bussu Bay because there'd been a break-in at the resort.

We'd been given the awful news that a body had washed up further along the coast, and we had to go and see if it was Drew. The trauma of the not knowing as we went up there, had been whisked away when we found it wasn't Drew. I'd been hopeful again that he might yet turn up.

Then we'd gone back to find the resort had been burgled. All the jewellery, money, passports and credit cards had been stolen. It then took weeks to sort out new passports and credit cards, and Jake almost lost his job. I did lose my job which was another level of stress, because I now had a baby to support. I didn't know how I was going to cope in many ways, especially since my parents were thousands of miles away and Drew's parents had died before I met him.

I had a very clear bump now and as it grew, the more scared I became about the future. I stepped out on to the pavement and felt a fluttering inside, deep in my stomach. Like butterflies.

'Oh my goodness,' I said to Jake.

'What? What's the matter?' he asked.

I grabbed his hand and placed it on my stomach. 'I just felt the baby move.'

We both stood still, waiting, waiting, waiting . . . There, it happened again.

'Wow,' Jake said. 'It's a baby, it's a real baby.'

'I know!' It was a real baby. For the first time since I'd found out I was pregnant it felt real. Like it was something that would actually happen. Tears sprang to my eyes. 'I wish Drew was here,' I said. 'He so wanted us to get married and have a baby. Even when I wasn't so sure, he was desperate for this. And now he's not here for it.'

'It'll be all right,' Jake said. 'I promise, it'll be all right.'

24 years ago

I sat in a hospital bed and stared down at my baby. She was perfect. Her dark brown skin was wrinkled and soft. Her lips were parted as she slept, and her long black eyelashes almost reached her cheeks.

Jake was collecting my parents from the airport and a few friends had promised to visit in the coming days.

I didn't want anyone, though. I wanted to go to a secret island with my baby and live there without anyone else. Not even Jake. Not even, I admitted to myself for a brief second, Drew. I wanted it to be just me and Nia, as I had named her, for ever.

Now

Jake curls his body around me and kisses my shoulder. I feel him growing hard against me and I know he'd like us to make love, to reconnect in a physical way, but I can't. I'm finding all of this too much. Too difficult. I thought I could handle it; I thought Nia getting married here might break the curse of weddings on Bussu Bay beach. But it is getting more and more difficult to stop myself crying. I live here all the time and it is fine – I have found a way to make peace with that. I avoid the beach as much as possible by staying inside the resort or walking into the village. But with Nia here, with her wedding so close, I have to confront what happened and I am struggling. All I want to do is curl up and disappear.

What Jake wants to do is make love. His kisses move lower, his hands start to caress my skin.

'I can't,' I blurt out. 'I'm sorry, I just can't.'

'That's OK,' he says and moves away. 'That's OK.'

It's not OK, I know that. He needs us to make love to feel we're connected because I can't say 'I love you' to him. I've never been able to say it to him, not when I feel so guilty all the time

19

about being with him instead of Drew. He accepts that, because I show him in other ways how I feel.

Jake moves to the other side of the bed and I can feel the emotional gap between us. I know what he needs, but I can't give it to him right now. I just can't.

6

Now

'And mind you do not move into the Honey-moon Suite when I am not here,' my mother tells her granddaughter. Mum and Dad are heading off to stay with friends near Accra, Ghana's capital city, for a few nights and will be back two days before the wedding.

I think it's all too much for them as well. Losing Drew in the sea broke Dad's heart. He felt responsible for not finding Drew, and Mum felt powerless to stop the pain I was going through. Nia's wedding, exciting as it is, has made us all a little jumpy and on edge. I think my parents are going visiting to keep their worries and fears away from her.

'Would I do that, Grandma?' Nia says with a pout.

'Does your daughter think I was born yesterday?' Mum asks me.

I shrug. I'm not taking sides in this one.

'I am a grown woman, you know?' Nia says. 'I can make my own decisions.'

'I know that, child,' Mum says. 'And that is why I have given Kwame and Edward strict instructions to call me the very second you start making those "own decisions".'

Nia's face is a picture. She glances at me, and I shrug at her as I mouth 'Lightweight' to remind her of what she said to me last night.

'Bye, Grandma,' she says when she realises I won't be helping her.

'Bye, bye, my darling granddaughter,' Mum says and receives Nia's hug. She turns to Marvin. 'I am still not sure about you.'

Marvin smiles. 'That's a huge improvement from last night. You've dropped the "yet", so I'm looking forward to you being a bit more sure about me.'

'Indeed,' Mum replies.

Jake is staring at me while the others go out to the car. He's driving my parents the 130 miles to visit their friends, and he'll probably stay there if I don't ask him to come back. I do want him to come back tonight. And I don't want him to come back tonight. I need some space to think. But I know that's selfish, and everything does feel better when he's here with me.

Jake waits and waits for me to ask him what

time he'll be back. When I don't ask, when he realises I'd like him to stay away, he inhales deeply and nods. 'All right,' he says. 'I'll see you in a couple of days.'

'Yes, I'll see you then.'

19 years ago

'Goodnight, then,' Jake whispered to me.

It was late on a Sunday night and he was about to drive back to London after spending the weekend with Nia and me in Brighton. Every weekend he drove down to be with us, and when Nia was younger, he'd often come during the week to help me. He would go to the shops for me. He would clean my flat. Sometimes he'd just sit with Nia so I could sleep – basically going above and beyond the call of duty as a friend to help me out.

We'd been watching something on the television and, as usual, I had fallen asleep long before he'd whispered goodbye.

'Don't go,' I whispered, with my eyes closed. I was half asleep, but I couldn't open my eyes and see his face if it meant he would be horrified by what I was saying. 'Stay, please.'

'I'll stay a bit longer,' he replied.

I opened my eyes and he was sitting on the floor beside the sofa. His face was so close to mine I could feel his breath on my cheek. We stared at each other in silence for a few seconds. 'Like I said, I'll stay a bit longer, but I do need to—' I cut him short by kissing him. He seemed unsure at first, probably shocked that I'd done this, and then he was kissing me too. Slowly, gently, he pushed me back on to the sofa and climbed on top of me, kissing me all the while. Our kiss deepened and I placed my hands on his face. A shiver of excitement ran through me at having his smooth, dark brown skin under my fingers, at having the weight of his body on top of me. It'd been so many years since I'd been this close to a man. I hadn't come even near to it since Drew.

Before either of us could change our minds, I reached for his flies and undid all the buttons, then pushed his trousers down over his hips. He groaned as I stroked the full, hard length of him.

I had fallen in love with Jake over the last few years. And it was obvious from the way he looked at me, the way he came to see us no matter what else was going on in his life, that he loved me too. But Drew and what happened to him was always between us.

Jake stared down into my eyes, and I was sure he could see what I was thinking: we needed to do this. It would lay to rest the ghost of Drew. Once we did this, maybe we would both stop being chained together with guilt and sadness, and we'd be able to move on and find someone else.

Jake reached up under my dress and moved aside my knickers. With his gaze locked on mine, he slowly pushed into me. We both moaned as we became one. I let go of his face and grabbed on to his shoulders to pull him closer, to make the whole of him the whole of me.

'I love you,' he whispered suddenly. 'I love you.'

I gripped him tighter, urged him to go deeper; I wanted more of him, all of him.

'I love you,' he whispered again, louder this time, as he pushed harder and faster. 'I love you, I love you, I love you, I lo—'

I put my lips on his to stop him saying it because I couldn't say it back. No matter how much I felt it, no matter how many times he said it, I couldn't say it back. 'I love you, I love you, I love you,' he kept murmuring against my lips. Over and over and over until finally he orgasmed and I orgasmed and we collapsed against each other on the sofa.

Eventually, Jake moved away from me and sat back to pull and do up his trousers. I straightened myself out as Jake climbed off the sofa and returned to sitting on the floor beside me, staring at the television. Nothing was said for long minutes and I wondered if we'd ever speak of this. Or if we would pretend it hadn't happened.

'I shouldn't have told you,' Jake finally said. 'You still miss Drew so much. I still miss him so much. He was my brother, you know? We grew up together, we did everything together. Double trouble, everyone called us. We looked alike, we were alike. My mum was always saying it was like she'd had twins, because she spent as much time telling him off as she did me. His mum said the same about me before she died. It makes sense we both wanted the same woman.'

I pulled my legs up towards my chest. He couldn't be saying what it sounded like he was saying . . .

'It'd only seriously happened once before, though, when we were in college. She didn't like either of us, so there was never any problem. Not until we met you.'

'But I met Drew in a club,' I said.

'I know. I was there. In fact, I met you more than once in that club. I used to go to see you.

26

It took me weeks to get up the courage to speak to you.'

'I was smashed out of my head most of the time. I never remembered anyone I met. I only really remembered Drew because I went home with him. Did I really meet you there?'

'Yes,' Jake replied. 'Well before Drew came with me. I was working up to asking for your number, so I could speak to you when you were sober, but then Drew came to the club that night and decided he liked you too. Since the woman we both liked in college, we'd always agreed that if we both like a woman, we both stay away. When my back was turned he went for you. Went home with you. We had a proper dust-up about it months later.'

'You fought over me?' I asked, horrified.

Jake hung his head in shame. 'It wasn't just about you. It was what he did. How he went about it. We'd agreed. We'd agreed that we wouldn't let anyone come between us again. And he just . . . I could've dealt with it if he'd left it as a one-night stand, but he didn't. He was out of order. After the dust-up, even he admitted that he'd been out of order. He offered to step back. But,' Jake shrugged, 'I could see you loved him. I just had to deal with the fact that he'd made a move when I was still thinking about it.'

Jake went on: 'When he died ... I hated myself. I'd spent so long secretly angry at him and secretly in love with you, I felt like I brought it on him. That I'd jinxed him.'

'I don't believe this,' I said.

I was reeling. It was all such a surprise, but was it? Did I really not know all those years ago that Jake might have had feelings for me? Drew, more than once, had accused me of having feelings for Jake. He said he'd seen us staring at each other. Once he even thought I'd slept with Jake because we'd both had our mobiles off at the same time. He'd only believed me when I broke down and begged him to end things if he truly thought I'd cheat on him. Maybe that was why Drew had been so possessive; maybe it wasn't just a way to control me and stop me from speaking to Jake or any other man, as I'd once told him. Maybe Drew thought that Jake still had feelings for me.

Jake stood up. 'Like I said, I shouldn't have told you. I'll understand if you don't want me to come over any more.'

I reached out and took his hand. 'Don't go,' I said. I may not have noticed before how he felt, but I knew now. And it wasn't as if I hadn't fallen for him.

I stood up too and led him to the bedroom.

Once I had shut the bedroom door behind us, I slowly took off my dress and dropped it on to the floor. Then, just as slowly, I lay back on the bed, waiting for him to take off his clothes.

I wanted to be with him, I decided.

Carefully, his eyes staring into mine the whole time, a now-naked Jake took off my knickers.

I wanted to be with someone I loved, I realised as he eased himself into me. I wanted to be with someone who, as I had just found out, had always loved me.

Now

I don't watch Jake and my parents drive away. Instead, I stand in our bedroom, feeling guilty. I should have asked him to come back. I shouldn't have just let him go like that. What if it's the last time I see him? What if something happens to him like it happened to Drew? He will have left thinking I don't love him. I've never said it. I've always told myself he knows how I feel and I don't need to spell it out. But what if I never see him again?

I reach for my mobile phone.

I love you, I type. **I love you so very much. You mean the world to me. I've spent so much**

of my life with you and you're everything to me. I hope you realise that. I hope you know that you are my everything. All my love, Tessa

I read those words over and over until they are seared into my brain. Until I can recite them off by heart. Slowly and carefully, I delete every single letter. I can't send him that. He'll expect me to say it, to hold him, to break through the barrier that's always between us.

I'll see you when you get back. X I send instead.

16 years ago

'Mum.' Nia had her serious voice on. She had obviously been mulling something over, and had decided that now was the time for her to share her thoughts with me. She was eight years old and a very deep thinker. In that way, she was more like Jake than Drew.

Every day, to me, she looked more like Drew, even though everyone else said she was exactly like me and not a bit like him. But, no matter what she looked like, she became more and more like Jake every day. She thought long and hard about things. She was always mindful of other people's feelings before her own. And the pair of them seemed to find so many of the same things funny, when I just didn't get the joke.

'Mum, I think you should marry Jake.'

Taken aback, I stared at my daughter. Jake had been living with us for nearly a year – before that, he was always around – so I didn't understand this sudden need in her for us to get married.

Nia knew Jake wasn't her father. She knew her dad had died before she was born, but she hadn't shown any interest in Drew. I had originally put a photo of him in her bedroom, but she'd asked me to take it down because she didn't like the strange man staring at her.

Whenever I tried to talk about him, she would literally walk away. 'Give her time,' Mum told me. 'He is not real to her, give her time; when she grows and becomes more curious about the world and her place in it, she will ask.'

She hadn't. She would ask all sorts of questions about all sorts of people – about her grandparents, about relatives who lived in Ghana. She would question Jake about his family, his siblings, about his relatives who lived in the Bahamas – but she never seemed to want to know about that person who helped create her.

I wondered if it was because, somewhere inside, she was hurt and angry that he wasn't here? That he had left her before she'd even had a chance to know him, and it upset her too much to allow him and the memory of him into her life.

'Why do you think I should marry your uncle Jake?' I replied.

'He's not my uncle. I've asked him over and over and he's told me all about his family, and zero times has he said anything that would mean he's my uncle.'

'All right, why should I marry Jake?'

'Because he's there.'

'Because he's *there*?'

'Yes. That's what you do. You meet someone who is there for you and you get married to them.'

'Where have you heard that?'

'You say it all the time on the phone to your friends. You say you love him because he's "there for me". And if you love him like that, that must mean you should get married.'

'It doesn't actually.'

Nia sighed and then pulled a face that basically said I was forcing her hand. 'Mum, if you get married to him, I can call him Daddy.'

I stared at her wide-eyed with shock. It hadn't occurred to me she might want to call him that.

She wasn't finished: 'I want a baby brother or

a baby sister. You need a mummy and daddy to make a baby.' She spoke very slowly as though I needed help to understand what she was saying. 'You are the mummy and, when you get married, Jake will be the daddy.'

'Jake might not want to get married. He might not want to give you a baby brother or sister.'

'He does. He told me.'

'OK, so that's not a problem,' I said.

'So are you going to marry him?' she asked.

'I don't think so, Nia.'

'Why not?'

'I don't want to get married again.'

'But you didn't get married last time, Mum,' she pointed out. 'My daddy died on the day you were meant to get married before I was born. But Jake didn't. And you didn't. So I think you should get married.'

'I'll think about it,' I said to stop her going on.

'OK, Mum.' She ran off to play, and then came back seconds later and threw her arms around me in the biggest huggle in the world. She was always the best at them.

7

Now

My daughter is the most laid-back bride in the world.

So far, she hasn't had a tantrum, hissy fit or even a cross word to say about the wedding plans. Adjoa, the housekeeper, begged me to let her plan the wedding. It was her dream to start a wedding-planning business and she wanted to practise on Nia. During the last few weeks Adjoa and my daughter have been in contact about the wedding via Messenger and email. Nia has said she'll show Adjoa and me her dress later but now they're going over those wedding ideas in person.

We sit in the library, a comfortable space with whitewashed walls and books and music CDs available for the guests to use. Instead of sitting on the big sofas and using the coffee tables, everything is spread on the tiled floor. So far, everything that Adjoa takes out to show them is met with squeals of delight from Nia and murmurs of approval from Marvin.

Her bouquet is a beautiful mix of red, orange, pink and white flowers, all native to different parts of Ghana. When Adjoa shows her the table designs, I think my daughter is actually going to explode with happiness.

'This is going to be the best beach wedding ever,' Nia squeals.

Adjoa's eyes widen in alarm and Marvin nudges his wife-to-be. Nia immediately remembers and looks at me, terrified that she's hurt me. 'Sorry, Mum,' she says.

'You're right, it will be the best beach wedding ever,' I say. 'It's going to be fantastic. I can't wait to give you away.'

'Erm . . . about that,' Nia says.

'Yes?'

'Well, I was kind of hoping that . . .'

Marvin rolls his eyes at his fiancée. 'She was hoping that you *and* Jake would give her away,' he says. 'That's if you don't mind.'

'Oh,' I say. 'Oh. I'm sure he'll be over the moon. And of course I don't mind.'

'You could always get married with us, you know?' Nia says with a giggle.

'You could always sleep in with Grandma and Grandpa when they come back, you know?' I reply.

'Point taken.'

35

Now

I'm using this opportunity of an empty resort to do some spring cleaning. Even though the three other cleaners and I do our best to keep the place sand-free and pristine, it's hard when there are guests constantly around.

While Marvin and Nia get ready to go to the beach, I've put on my overalls and tied my hair up in a scarf ready to start in the reception area.

When I first arrived to take over running Bussu Bay, most of the staff didn't believe a girl like me, who had been brought up in England, could be anything but spoiled and difficult. I had to prove them wrong. I had to muck in, pick up after the guests, clean toilets, go to fetch water if that was what was needed, as well as manage the place. Slowly, they accepted me.

When I get down under the desk, I realise that whoever was in charge of this area last week needs a good talking-to. A small dune of sand seems to have collected between the large driftwood-carved reception desk and the wall. There are cobwebs between the filing cabinet and wall, and I can see a line of dust all along the skirting board. *Not good enough*, I think as I pull the cloth from the front pocket of my overall and start to wipe away the dust. 'Not good enough at all,' I mumble.

'Oh, excuse me,' a male voice says.

I jump a little at the interruption and bang my head on the desk. 'Ouch!' I say and rub at my head. I hadn't heard a car draw up so wasn't expecting anyone. And this person is speaking English with a British accent.

'Oh, I'm so sorry, did I startle you?'

My whole body slows down at that voice. I'm not aware any more that I am kneeling on a tiled floor. I can't feel the buzzing heat that has been rising with each passing minute. I can't feel the tummy rumble of a missed breakfast. I can't feel anything but the swirling in my head as that voice filters into my ears. 'Can you tell me where I can find Tessa?' he continues. 'She runs the place now, apparently.'

Slowly, slowly, slowly, I back out from under the desk into the wide reception area. Slowly, slowly, slowly, I stand on my shaky legs.

Slowly, slowly, slowly, I look at the man who is standing just inside the big arched doorway that welcomes people to Bussu Bay. The place where I live. The place where I lost the love of my life on my wedding day.

I stare at the man in front of me. And I blink. Once. Twice. Three times.

37

The man in front of me looks nothing like the man I lost twenty-four years ago, of course. This man has wrinkles in the dark brown skin around his eyes, the man I lost had smooth skin. This man has a neatly cut and styled Afro, while the man I lost had an almost shaved head. This man has a scar to the left of his nose, while the man I lost had the exact same-size scar in the exact same place.

This man is the man I lost. Of course he is.

'Tessa,' he says. 'Hi.'

27 years ago

'Weren't we supposed to be a one-night stand?' Drew said to me. I was always dazzled by his smile, by the strength of his arms around me, the look in his eyes when he stared at me.

'I do believe that was what we agreed when we went home together, yes,' I replied.

This was our sixth date after meeting two weeks earlier in a west London nightclub. Everything was a wonderful, giddy blur of meeting up, going for drinks and spending the night in bed. He would buy me flowers, tell me how beautiful I was, tell me how much he adored me.

'What a difference two weeks make,' he said

as we stood on Brighton station, waiting for the train that would take us up to London.

'I know. From one-night stand to all of this. This must be some kind of record,' I said.

'No, this must be love. You know, I think our destiny was shaped by the stars,' he said to me. 'And I'm going to marry you one day . . . You and that cute little nose of yours.'

'My nose isn't interested,' I replied. 'But the rest of me—' He cut me off by kissing me. Long and slow. Of all the things he did, the kissing was the best part.

Now

'I can't believe it's you,' Drew says to me. 'I mean . . . It's so good to see you, Tessa.'

I'm staring at a ghost. With all the wedding planning and thinking about him, I must have imagined up a version of him. Perfectly aged and asking for me.

In the early days of losing Drew, Jake and I would talk about this, about how we would sometimes see Drew in a crowd. We would catch a glimpse of his profile, the back of his head, his distinctive walk, the way he held himself, and we would think it was him. I'd often move to call to him, to try to get to him . . . then I would remember the night spent on the beach, watching, waiting. And I would pull myself together and tell myself it wasn't possible.

'I guess you must be a bit shocked,' he says.

He's alive. He's alive! Drew cheated death and he's found a way back to me. I almost run at him, throw my arms around his neck and kiss every single part of him. He's here. I can't believe he's here. I have so many questions; I have so many things to tell him. I can't believe the thing I have wished for all these years has come true.

I open my mouth to speak and 'DAD!' Marvin shouts, appearing in the reception area. He is dressed in a shorty wetsuit and looks ready to go out surfing. 'What are you doing here?'

'Dad?' I manage.

'Yes, sorry, Tessa – I mean, Ms Dannall – I mean, Nia's mum. This is my dad, Andrew.'

8

Now

'Nia! Nia!' Marvin calls over his shoulder. 'My dad's arrived!'

He then returns to focusing on his father. 'What are you doing here? Aren't you, like, three days early?'

Marvin's father does not take his eyes off me as he speaks. 'Yes, we're early. Your mother couldn't wait any longer. She wanted to top up her tan before the wedding. Well that was the official excuse, but the real one is that she missed you. I told her we should call ahead, but she wouldn't hear of it. She wanted to surprise you.'

'Where is she?' Marvin asks.

'Outside, refusing to move from the car until I make sure we have the biggest room in the resort.' He was always good at that, speaking to one person while concentrating on another.

'Nia!' Marvin calls again, louder this time. 'Nia, my mum and dad are here!'

I hear sounds of my daughter approaching

and I still can't take my eyes off the man in front of me.

This can't be happening. Because if it is, that means that Marvin and Nia are . . . *Please let this be a mistake*, I think as Nia appears in the reception area dressed in a summer dress with a large sun hat in her hands.

'Mr Parsons, how lovely to see you,' she says very politely.

'Andrew, please – I've told you before.' Nia goes to him and kisses him on the cheek and I feel myself wobble. *This can't be happening.*

'Have you met my—' Nia stops talking when I sway so violently I have to grab the desk for support. 'Mum, are you OK?' she asks and dashes to me.

'I'm fine, I'm fine,' I say and try to wave her away. All the while I can feel Drew's eyes on me. I can feel all their eyes on me now. I'm showing myself up, I'm showing my daughter up. But what is happening is so horrific it's a wonder I haven't started throwing up.

'Andrew!' Marvin's mother barks from the doorway to get her husband's attention.

Her sunglasses and clothes look very expensive. Her auburn hair is cut and styled in a shape that she obviously knows suits her, and her sandals look like real designer shoes instead of cheap knock-offs. Nia had told me her future in-laws were very posh and it shows.

'Yes, darling?' Drew finally stops staring at me and turns to face his wife.

'Exactly how long do you intend to leave me sitting out there? The taxi driver is getting rather annoyed.'

'I'll go and pay him and bring in our bags,' Drew says meekly. He was never like that with me. He was usually quite forceful. I watch him leave the building, wondering why he is so different with this woman.

'Darling!' Marvin's mum says, throwing open her arms. He grins at his mother and walks into a hug. 'I couldn't wait any longer to see you,' she explains. 'Your father said it'd be fine not to call ahead. He wanted to surprise you. I hope you're not too cross that we arrived so early.'

'Well, I don't mind, obviously, but you'll have to talk to Nia's mum. It's her resort.' Marvin points towards me. 'Mum, this is Tessa, Nia's mum . . . Tessa, this is my mum, Ellen.'

When I do nothing but stare at Ellen, Drew's wife, my daughter nudges me to go to shake her hand. I leave the safety of the desk and go towards her, forcing a smile on my face.

'Pleased to meet you,' we say at the same time.

Neither of us moves to shake hands, though. It feels like an instant mutual dislike has sprung up between us, but for what reason, I don't know. I just know that there is something about her that I don't like. From the way she fake-smiles at me, I think she feels the same.

Behind her, I can hear Drew returning with their bags and I don't want to see him again. I need time to think. Because I will have to tell Nia and Marvin they are brother and sister. They only share half a bloodline, but it is still too much when they want to get married.

'It's . . . it's so lovely to see you,' I force myself to say with a smile. 'I will just go and see if we can find you a made-up room. Do excuse me.' Before anyone can protest, I disappear off down the corridor without looking back.

Now

'*Ma'am?*' Kwame asks in Akan, the main Ghanaian language. '*Are you all right?*' I am leaning against the wall by the kitchen door, trying to catch my breath. Trying to breathe and trying to work out what to do. I need to talk to Jake. And I need to talk to Nia. And Marvin. And of course I need to talk to Drew. Before I can talk

44

to anyone else, I need to talk to Drew. But, after all this time, after all the many ways I've longed for him to return, right now, talking to him is the last thing I want to do.

I stand upright, pull myself together. 'Marvin's parents have arrived,' I say to Kwame, trying to sound normal. 'Can you show them to the Grand Suite, please? I cleaned it myself two days ago, so it will only need fresh water and for you to light the mosquito lamp in the corner.'

We've built up a good friendship over the time I've been here, and Kwame is like the little brother I never had. (Edward, who also lives here, is a bit more serious and formal with me than Kwame.) Kwame looks me over, still worried about how I am behaving. He doesn't know me like this. He wasn't around for my wedding, and most of the time I am happy. I sing while I work, I dance if there's room, I sit in the kitchen with them and we tell each other silly stories. He's never seen me this close to breaking down. 'Are you sure you are all right, Miss Tessa?' Kwame asks in English.

I nod and smile at him. 'A bit too much sun and a bit too little to eat.'

'If you are sure,' he replies and then leaves to do as he's told.

If Marvin's mother really does need to have

the biggest room, the Grand Suite should make her happy. It is the only set of rooms – living space, small kitchen, bedroom and bathroom with shower – that is not physically connected to the main Bussu Bay complex. There is a little pebbly path that leads to the main building. It is just long enough to make people think twice about simply getting up and going over to the main part on a whim. If I keep them out there, they may sit down and realise how tired they are. They'll hopefully then grab a nap for a few hours and I will be able to have time to think. To work out how I'm going to tell Nia about all of this.

Every time I think about what my daughter is about to go through, I feel sick. I want to grab her and whisk her away. Take her to an island where it will be just the two of us together, for ever. Just like I wished it could be when she was first born. Every time I think about what my daughter is about to go through, I wish there was a way to take away her pain and make it mine.

I take another deep breath, slowly lower myself to the ground and rest my forehead on my hands. How could Drew do this? He must have worked out who Nia was the second he heard where they were getting married. Surely. He couldn't have believed it was a huge coincidence, could he? No one would be that naive. Surely? Of course he wasn't. He asked for me by name when he arrived. He knew it was me living here, he knew she was my daughter. So why would he just show up here? Why wouldn't he call or something beforehand?

Was it so this would all be a big surprise for me? So that I would see him and would be so overcome by the fact he was still alive that I wouldn't question what happened all those years ago?

Was he really so selfish that he would risk his son's wedding by just showing up and hoping for the best? The me who lost him on the beach all those years ago would have said no, absolutely not. But the me who lived with him up until that point, the me who was constantly putting aside her real feelings so I could remember how much I loved him, would have, eventually, said yes: he is that selfish. Because that me knew that when Drew wanted something, he didn't let anything stand in his way.

26 years ago

'Now there, sugar plum, if I give you this hot lemon and honey that I have so lovingly prepared, what will I get in return?' Drew asked me.

47

I could barely lift my head from the pillow and I couldn't talk much without coughing, so I couldn't really answer Drew. It was no fun being around a sick person, I knew that. But when you're the sick person, it's no fun having someone try to make you barter for your cold remedy. 'My eternal gratitude,' I croaked before I reached for a tissue from the box beside the bed.

'You can do better than that,' Drew said with a mischievous smile dancing around his lips.

'Really can't.'

'Yes, you can,' he replied. He put the cup on the floor beside the bed and then moved the tissues and the antibiotics I needed to take soon, as well as the painkillers, out of reach.

'Please,' I said tiredly. I really did not want to play games. My chest was on fire most of the time when I wasn't coughing, and my throat – which had showed signs of developing tonsillitis, the doctor said – seemed to be getting worse, not better.

Drew pulled back the covers. 'I think a little action will be more than enough to show me how grateful you are,' he said.

'I'm ill,' I groaned.

'You can still talk so you can't be that ill,' he replied. He reached for my pyjama bottoms.

'Please don't, Drew,' I said. 'Please.'

He tutted loudly. 'Fine,' he said. 'I'll find someone else to play with if you won't.' He got up, took the drink, the painkillers and my antibiotics and left the room. A few minutes later I heard him leave the flat. It took all my strength to get out of bed and down the corridor to the kitchen. Once there, I found he'd emptied out the drink and had taken the antibiotics and painkillers with him.

I didn't have the energy to make it back to bed, so had to sink to the floor in the kitchen to wait until I felt well enough to move. While I waited I cried and cried and cried.

Now

I don't like to think about when Drew wasn't nice to me.

Even back then I would spend a lot of time pretending it hadn't happened or that it wasn't so bad, because those times didn't make up a fair picture of who he truly was. He was mostly good to me. It was just that, when he wasn't good to me, it was extreme. It was *nasty*. When he wasn't nice to me, it was never something tame – it was always something that ended with me in floods of tears, feeling broken. But it wasn't all the time, which is why I didn't like to think about it – let alone talk about it. The nasty him wasn't the real him.

My mobile phone rings in my pocket, knocking me out of my daydream and into the present.

Jake calling, says the screen. I accept the call and say hello.

'Hey,' Jake's voice says. 'We got here in good time. Roads were clear, hardly any stops. All cool with you, babe?'

I feel myself unclench when I hear his voice. He's trying to sound normal, to ignore the atmosphere there was between us before he left. And I love him for it. I love him for being so normal.

'You have to come back,' I tell him.

'Your parents' friends are about to put out lunch. They've been making palm-nut soup and pounding *fufu* since dawn. I can't just leave.'

'Drew,' I say quietly, carefully. It's the first time I've said his name out loud in years. There's never been any need. When I am talking to Jake, Drew has always been 'him' or 'he' and that has been enough.

I can hear Jake take a deep breath in, shocked that I've said his name. Surprised that I've said it so calmly. 'What about him?' Jake says with a frosty tone.

'He's here.'

Jake gives a short, humourless laugh. 'Right,' he says. 'That's not funny.'

'I'm not joking. I'm not—' I start to hyperventilate, as the truth hits me. He's not dead. Drew's not dead. He was never dead. I have mourned him for half my life, and he's been alive all along. 'Wedding,' I manage. 'Wedding. Here. For. Wedding.'

'I'm on my way,' I hear Jake say as I drop my phone, not caring that the screen cracks when it hits the ground.

Drew's alive. Drew's alive and he's here, about to ruin my and my daughter's lives all over again.

9

Now

On the other side of the set of buildings that makes up Bussu Bay Resort and Water Sports Centre, a little further along the beach, there is an area where the greenery and palm trees start to encroach on the sand. That's because, behind it, there is a series of caves that you can only get to by a very rocky path. Some of the rocks on the path are so large that you have to step up on top of them to get over them.

When I was little we would come here from England to stay with my grandparents for the six-week summer holiday. My parents would bring me to play on this area of the beach, while they were making their plans to build Bussu Bay. Work started when I was ten, and finished when I was about seventeen. A year after that, my parents left England to come here, to open their resort and change the lives of everyone in the community.

Sometimes my cousins would be here too, but

mostly I was on my own. I'd go off exploring, and would spend hours in these caves, drawing pictures on the sand floors, running my fingers along the cool, damp walls. I would bring toys and hold tea parties with bits and pieces I found on the beach. The older I got, the more time I would spend in the caves just reading.

I walk down to the caves now, hoping I can disappear for hours like I used to when I was a child. Hoping that I will be able to run my hands along the clammy walls and conjure up a time in my life before Drew, before the death that was not a death.

I have walked around this cave, one of my favourites, for a while now and feel calmer for it. I need to decide how to tell Nia and Marvin.

It took me a while to pull myself together after the panic attack outside the kitchen. By the time I was able to go back inside, Marvin told me his mum had gone to unpack and then have a nap, and Nia and Marvin were going to help make lunch before they went to the beach. Drew was nowhere to be seen, and Marvin had explained his dad had gone to explore the area.

I'd stared at Nia and Marvin, knowing I should tell them they were brother and sister, but the words would not come out of my mouth. This is why I have come to the caves – to gather strength and get my head together.

As I stand here, I know that with every hour that passes, the more I am colluding in what is going on with my daughter. I have to summon up my courage to tell her and Marvin. I close my eyes and stand very still. I don't want to do this.

'I thought I might find you here.' Drew's voice echoes on the stone around us. 'I guessed this would still be your most favourite place in the whole of Ghana.'

I open my eyes but I do not know what to say to him. Well, I do. I have lots of things to say to him: *What are you doing here? Did you fake your own death? Do you have any idea what you've done to the last twenty-four years of my life? How could you even bring yourself to come back here after the last time? Do you still love me? Did you ever love me?* I have many, many things to say to him, but nothing will come out.

'Aren't you going to say anything?' Drew asks me.

I can't do this, I realise. I can't stand in here, one of my special safe spaces, the place I shared with only him – not even Nia knows about this place, let alone Jake – and talk to him. I just can't.

I start to leave and he stands in my way, stops me from exiting. Our bodies almost but don't quite touch. He brings his face down towards mine, leans in close and lowers his voice.

'I didn't want to leave you,' Drew says. 'But I had no choice. Jake tried to kill me.'

25 years ago

I dried my eyes before I picked up the intercom. I'd tried to ignore the doorbell, but the person wouldn't stop pressing it, so I guessed they knew I was in. I cleared my throat and said, 'Hello?' into the receiver.

'It's me,' Jake said.

'Ah, Jake, sorry, Drew's not here.'

'It was you I came to see.'

Short of being rude, I had to let him in. I looked a horror as I'd been crying most of the morning. I'd been crying so much and looked so dreadful, I'd had to take the day off work. 'Come up,' I said and buzzed him in.

'Why aren't you at work?' he asked the second he saw me. 'I called to see if you and Drew wanted to meet up tonight and they said you were off sick.' He peered at me. 'Are you really sick? Because you just look like you've been crying.'

'I'm tired,' I replied. Not sick, just tired. I was tired of where I was with Drew. For some reason, we just couldn't get on right then. We had the wedding booked and he'd been talking about us having a baby. The problem was, I was enjoying my job in marketing – there was a real chance of promotion, and I wasn't sure I wanted a baby at that time. Drew didn't understand that. He just saw it as me not being as committed to him as he was to me.

'Tired of what?' Jake asked.

'It's complicated,' I replied.

It *was* complicated. Because Drew wanted it all – *right now*. He wanted the big wedding, the baby, but also he wanted to open a bar – and he wanted me to ask my parents for the money to pay for it. He had this idea that, because they'd opened a hotel, they were rich and they should be helping us out more. Both his parents had died, so he felt my folks should be willing to finance our dreams. I'd never relied on my parents for anything and I had always paid for my own lifestyle, so there was no way I was going to start asking them for money now. This was what caused most of the arguments between Drew and me: I wouldn't ask, and he took that as a sign that I didn't want him to succeed in life.

That was why I was tired: we kept having the

same arguments and it was wearing me down. But I loved him. He sometimes made me feel incredible and I knew this patch would eventually pass, but it was exhausting. And I couldn't talk to anyone about it, because it would make Drew sound awful. And when we were through this awful period, when things were perfect again, the person I had told those things to wouldn't forget; they'd continue to think badly of him.

'If he's being out of order, tell me and I'll sort it with him,' Jake said.

'It's not like that,' I told Jake. We hadn't moved from the corridor, which was probably a good thing, because I could tell Drew in all honesty that Jake had just popped by but hadn't set even a foot inside.

'I'll kill him if he hurts you,' Jake said. 'I've told him that – if he hurts you, I'll kill him.'

'He wouldn't hurt me,' I replied. Those other times – like the time he took away my medicine, the time he grabbed my wrist and squeezed, the time he threw a mug and it smashed near my head – those weren't anything serious. They didn't count as hurting me. 'And you mustn't say things like that, Jake. Someone might overhear and take it the wrong way.'

'There's only one way to take that,' he said. 'He's always treated his girlfriends badly – I thought he'd stopped with you. But if he's making you cry and miss work, then he needs sorting out. And he knows I'll do it.'

'It sounds like you've ignored how he treated his other girlfriends, and you're only drawing a line with me,' I said.

'I am. I should have stopped him a long time ago, but, yes, I've told him if he hurts you, I'll end him.'

'Why me?' I asked.

He put his head to one side, went to say something, then seemed to change his mind. 'Because you're my friend too.'

I wanted to hug Jake but didn't – I couldn't risk Drew catching me touching him, let alone holding him. 'Thanks, Jake. It makes me feel safe to know you're looking out for me, but there really is no need.' I smiled at him.

He looked again like he was about to say something, but again changed his mind. 'Take care of yourself, all right?'

'I will,' I replied. 'I will.'

10

Now

I'm frozen as I remember that conversation I had with Jake all those years ago. Six months later and Drew was dead as far as I was concerned. Six months later and Jake could very well have done what he'd threatened to do.

'It's true,' Drew says to my silence. 'He's always wanted you, and that day, out in the sea, he saw his chance to get rid of me for ever so he could have you, and he took it. And he almost did it – he almost killed me.'

I give my head a shake. 'You are lying. Jake would never do that. No one I know would do that. I can't believe you're lying about him. He's a good man and in all these years he's never—'

'Good man?' Drew laughs nastily. 'You really don't know him at all, do you?'

'I'm not listening to any more of this nonsense,' I say. And it is nonsense. Despite that conversation Jake and I had six months before Drew disappeared. Despite what Jake said about feeling guilty about what happened to Drew the first time we made love, I know this is nonsense.

I move to leave and Drew takes me in his arms. Encircles me with his hold and keeps me still, stares down at me until I stare up at him. For a moment, I'm back in the past, in those moments where he made me feel so very loved, so very safe. He lowers his head, his lips aiming for mine, and for a second I almost melt. I almost relax enough for him to kiss me. Because, with Drew, kissing was always the best part of it all . . .

Instead of melting, though, I push him away. 'Get your hands off me!' I snarl at him. *How dare he!* How *dare* he show up here and even think about touching me, let alone holding me, moving to kiss me. I take a step back from him. Then another. 'Don't you dare touch me again!'

'I know you don't want to listen to what happened, but you're going to have to,' Drew says. 'Then you can tell me if you think Jake is a good man or not. Then you'll understand why I had to do what I did.'

I shake my head. 'We've got bigger problems than this,' I say to him. 'And I don't want to hear anything you've got to say.'

'You have to,' he replies.

'I don't. I don't want to hear anything from you.'

'Why? Scared of what you'll find out about Mr Perfect?' Drew sneers.

'I know he didn't do anything to you, let alone try to kill you, so no, I'm not worried about what you'll say. I just want to get back to—'

'If you're not scared of what you'll hear, then why won't you listen?'

'Because—' I cover my face with my hands. This was what it was like arguing with him. Circular; round and round. Never enough to say no; always having to justify myself and my reasons or opinions. On and on until it was easier to just give in and let him get it over with. 'All right, go on then.'

I fold my arms across my chest and stare at the cave wall to the right of his head and wait for him to speak.

When a couple of minutes pass and he hasn't spoken, I turn to look at him. 'I can't believe how beautiful you still are,' he says softly.

He hasn't aged much at all. Yes, he has wrinkles around his eyes, but his skin is still that gorgeous chestnut brown. His large eyes still have that sparkle when he looks at me. And his lips, so full and— 'Start talking or I am leaving,' I say.

'All right, look, there was so much going on.

61

The minister was about to start the wedding service when we heard the woman shouting that her child was in the sea, remember?'

I nod. Of course I remember. I remembered every single second of it.

'And remember me and Jake and a couple of the busboys began to run to the water, because we had to save him? The busboys and Jake were much stronger swimmers than me, but for some reason I managed to get to him first. I don't know if you could see that from the beach?' We couldn't – the horizon and the position of the sun seemed to obscure what was happening out there. We all knew there were people in the sea, but we couldn't see what was going on.

'The little boy was flailing about, but I managed to hook my arm around his waist to keep him upright, when I saw Jake coming towards me. I knew it'd be all right then, because by that point I was exhausted. I wasn't sure I'd make it back to shore, especially while carrying the little boy. Jake swam up to me. "Thank God you're here, bruv," I shouted to him. And he looked about, checking, I realised later, to see if anyone was around – then he punched me in the face.

'I wasn't expecting that, and I let go of the boy. Jake took him, and I was all over the place, holding on to my nose and trying to keep afloat.

And then I felt Jake's hand on my head and he was pushing me under.'

'I don't believe that! Any of it. You're lying.'

'I'm not, Tessa, I'm not.' He points to his face. 'You can see where my nose doesn't look the same – he broke it when he punched me. I couldn't breathe. He was holding my head under and I was trying to breathe and my nose was agony.'

'So he was doing all this while holding on to a distressed, half drowned child, was he?'

'Yes. Don't you think I know how ridiculous it sounds? He did it. The busboys must have got closer to us, because he gave one last push under and then kicked me as he started to swim off. It was only a little kick, but after everything else he'd done, I couldn't fight any more. I let go and allowed myself to sink. There was nothing else I could do.

'I must have passed out because when I came round, I was on a beach way, way down the coastline. I didn't remember what had happened first of all. And when I did, first thing I did was get up and try to work out where I was. My nose was agony and I was confused. I walked for a while but I was so weak. Bits of what happened kept coming to me in flashes. I eventually came to a hotel and there was hardly anyone around except Ellen. She told me that everyone had gone to search for someone who had gone missing in the sea. She was a model and they'd been on a shoot the day before, but now most of them had gone to help search. I knew it was me they were looking for. But after what had happened with Jake, I knew no one would believe me, and it'd be only a matter of time before he tried again.'

'Can you hear yourself? "Tried again"? You've been watching too much television.'

'I knew you wouldn't believe me. Ellen did. But then, she saw the state of my broken nose; she hadn't been charmed by Jake like you and everyone else had. She agreed to help me. She let me stay in her room while I worked out what I was going to do.'

'Oh, I'll bet she let you stay in her room. How long was it before you were in her bed?' I say.

'It wasn't like that. How could I even think of being with another woman when I was meant to marry you? I rested in her room for a couple of days to let things settle down. I knew that if I could just talk to you alone, explain what had happened, you'd know that Jake was dangerous. We could start the wedding again. I snuck back to Bussu Bay to see you, and what did I find? You and Jake. He didn't even wait a week before he was all over you.'

'He was not all over me, he was comforting me,' I reply. 'I was devastated, he was devastated, he was looking after me.'

'I knew he would never leave your side, and I wasn't sure what he'd do if he knew his plan hadn't worked. I was scared, really scared that he'd try to harm you as well. He was completely obsessed with you, I realised. I knew if I could get to England—'

'How exactly did you get to England?' I cut in. 'Considering your passport and all your money were at Bussu Bay?'

'Ellen suggested we stage a break-in – have a few things stolen, including my passport, and then I could go home.'

'That was you?' I am horrified.

'No, no, not me. Ellen arranged it with a couple of the local lads – told them they could keep everything they stole except my passport. They must have gone too far. I'm so sorry.'

'You're sorry? They stole pretty much everything. Jewellery, money, the plane tickets home, my passport, my parents' passports, Jake's passport and plane tickets. All our British credit and debit cards. It was another nightmare added on to the one I was already living. We went through all of that so you could get your passport?'

'They weren't meant to do that. They were

supposed to only take a few things and my passport. Oh God, I had no idea.'

'It took weeks to sort everything out because Jake and I had no real ID. Weeks we were stuck here without any way of getting home to England, but you just went home without looking back.'

'That's not true! I was terrified – for me and you. I knew if I could get to England I'd be safe. I would contact you, and we could go to the police together.'

'And tell them that ridiculous story? Yeah, right.'

'Tessa, you don't know him like I do. He becomes obsessed with someone, and then anyone who's involved with them becomes a rival that he has to destroy.'

'Do you really think anyone is going to believe this stuff?'

'I didn't know how obsessed he could get, not until we fell out about this girl in college. He started a fist-fight with me over her. A proper knock-down brawl, it was. Over some girl who, it turned out, wasn't even interested in either of us.'

'So why did you stay friends with him then?'

'Because we've got a history. You don't let girls come before your mates. And anyway, afterwards he came up with this pact that, if we both liked a girl, neither of us would go out with her. And we stuck to that. Until you. And when I got with you, he attacked me again. That second time went way beyond anything I'd ever known from him before. He gave me a real pasting.

'Afterwards he said he could have handled it if it was a one-night stand, but me going out with you was all kinds of wrong. He said he was so angry and he wanted to hurt me. I had to beg him to let me keep dating you.

'I was going to tell the police everything, tell them what he did to me, and then we would both be safe. But you didn't come back for weeks. I thought you'd decided to stay in Bussu Bay with your parents. I knew I couldn't go back to our old flat until you were home because I wanted Jake to think I was dead so he wouldn't hurt you. Instead, I went to stay with Ellen and her parents in the countryside. She was so generous. She paid for my flight home and made sure someone looked at my nose properly when we got back. She even suggested I changed my name a bit, so no one could find me. By the time I found out that you'd come back to Brighton—'

'Let me guess,' I interrupt. 'By the time you found out that I'd come back to Brighton, you'd realised you had feelings for Ellen and decided it was best all round if I CONTINUED TO THINK YOU WERE DEAD!' I scream at him.

'No, no, it wasn't like that,' he says quickly, trying to calm me down. 'By the time you got back, I came to see you and he was there. Jake. And you were pregnant. I watched the two of you. I remember it clearly: you had both just come out of our flat and you took his hand and put it on your stomach to feel the baby moving, I think. And I realised that with me out of the way, he'd got what he wanted: you and now a baby.

'I knew there was no way on Earth you'd believe what he'd done, not when you were carrying his child. So I went away, praying that now he had a baby and the woman he'd always wanted, he'd settle down and you two could be happy. I knew that, if I popped up in your lives again, I would be putting you and probably your child at risk.

'I didn't get together properly with Ellen until months later. I'd started working in her father's business by then but, when we discovered Marvin was on the way, we had to speedily get married.' He takes a step forward until he is close to me. 'I couldn't believe it when Marvin told us where he and Nia wanted to get married, and that his fiancée's family owned this place. It was like everything had come full circle. I knew

I could finally set the record straight. I could finally see you again.

'I wasn't prepared, though, for all the emotions that I felt when we got here. And then, when I saw you again . . .' He stops talking. Then lowers his voice to say, 'I still love you.'

Lies – it's all lies. But then, there are bits that sound like the truth. Bits that remind me of conversations with Jake that could mean . . . *No. It's all lies. It has to be. Jake isn't a killer. And besides . . .*

'There's only one little problem,' I say as I push past Drew, making for the entrance to the cave.

'What's that?' he asks.

'Nia isn't Jake's daughter.'

'What? What are you saying?'

'She's not Jake's daughter – she's yours.'

Drew's eyes almost bulge out of his head. 'But that means . . .'

'Yes, that means your daughter is going to marry your son. Because you were a coward all those years ago and because you slunk away, instead of confronting Jake like you should have done if your story is true, your son is going to marry our daughter.'

11

Now

It seems a million times worse now I've said it out loud.

It is a horrible, horrible thing that is happening to Nia and Marvin. I don't know how Nia will deal with it. Or Marvin. The thought of it, all the times they'd ... My poor daughter. My poor, poor little girl.

I run for the cave exit, and stumble as I hit the rocky path that leads down through the greenery to the beach. I stumble on some of the bigger rocks before I hit the sand.

As soon as my flip-flops make contact with the hot, yellow sand, I start to run back to the resort.

I don't know what I'm going to do when I get there, what I'm going to say, but I have to tell her. Now. I can't leave it a moment longer than necessary. Listening to Drew talk has shown me what happens when you are a coward. When you decide to put yourself first and forget the possible hideous outcomes for other people.

'Tessa!' I can hear Drew calling behind me. 'Tessa! Wait! We need to talk about this.'

I push my legs harder, force them to run faster. I don't want to hear what he has to say. I listened to him just now and it has made everything a lot worse. When I first saw he was alive I thought that, perhaps, he'd lost his memory. That he didn't know about me and had gone on with life not knowing that I was waiting for him. But no, that wasn't the case. He'd been alive, he'd been well, he'd known all about me and he hadn't come for me. He had lied, and then he had convinced himself he didn't need to come back because I was with someone else.

That was the truth of it. It was easier for him to stay away, to start again, to let me grieve. Drew was a coward. A selfish coward. If it was true that Jake was a thug and capable of murder, then Drew had shown his weakness quite clearly by not even trying to get me away from him. He had just left me to my fate.

I do not want to talk to him, to listen to what he has to say, because I know it will be the coward's way out of this mess.

'Tessa! I need to talk to you!' Drew screams.

He sounds closer. He's faster than me, probably fitter. To my left, I can see the hotel buildings coming up, and I push myself, dig deep to make it. I start to turn towards safety but Drew catches up to me. He grabs me and pulls me to a standstill.

'Let go of me!' I cry and try to tug my arm free. Which makes him grab both of my arms and grip me tighter. 'Let go!' I shout again.

'We have to think about this,' he shouts back at me. His grip on me increases as I try to wrestle myself free. 'We can't just march in there and tell them all this. It will destroy them.'

'Let go!' I scream.

I remember once, not long after we got together, Drew and I were on the main bit of Victoria station and he'd been faffing about, which made us miss the train back to Brighton. I made a comment about it and suddenly he grabbed my forearm in a steel-like grip. He whispered in a low scary voice not to talk to him like that. When I told him he was hurting me, he increased his grip and told me to stop making a scene. He only let me go when two guys nearby told him to. Drew had immediately apologised and said he was out of order, and wouldn't do it again. But I knew, deep down, that I had to be careful when challenging him, that I had to think twice about criticising him – because I'd been given a glimpse of what could happen if I did.

'Let me go!' I shout again now, which makes him grip me even harder.

'You need to listen to me,' he snarls. 'You need to listen to me about what we're going to do.'

Using all my strength I try to pull myself away, trying to free myself from him. Suddenly he lets me go and I fall back on to the sand. 'Will you listen!' he screams. But before he can say anything else, I see Jake launch himself at Drew and the pair of them crash down on to the sand too. They start to fight, throwing sand up as they roll around. And then Nia and Marvin come running up the beach, closely followed by Kwame and Edward.

Marvin goes to intervene but Kwame holds him back, rightly not wanting him to get involved or hurt. I'm frozen where I sit, the sun beating down on us, watching this horror.

'Stop it!' Nia screams. 'Stop it! What are you doing? Just stop it! Dad, Dad, please just stop it.'

That seems to get through to them and they break apart and look at her.

'What are you doing, Dad?' Nia asks, through her sobs. 'Why are you behaving like this?' Jake, of course – she's talking to Jake. She's never called him that, not in all the years we've been together. I always took it as her way of making a point about me not marrying him. 'Dad, why are you trying to ruin my wedding?'

Drew screws up his face as he looks at my daughter. 'Wait. You know I'm your father?' he asks.

Everyone stops moving, probably stops breathing too. 'What did you say?' Nia whispers.

'Nothing, nothing,' Drew says as he realises Nia was calling Jake 'Dad'.

'Mum?' Nia says to me. 'Mum, what's going on?'

The shock and pain in her voice make me stand up. I go to her, try to take her in my arms, but she steps away. 'What's going on?' she asks again.

I can almost hear Drew silently willing me to make something up. To spare him this by lying for him.

'Nia, I'm sorry,' I say. 'I didn't want you to find out like this.'

'Are you trying to ruin it for me because your wedding went so wrong?' she asks me.

'No, no, of course not,' I reply.

'I don't believe you. You've been weird ever since I told you we wanted to get married here.'

'Nia, it's not that, I promise you.' I try to take her hands in mine but she snatches hers away. 'I didn't want you to find out like this,' I state.

'So it's true? He's—?' Her voice cuts out.

'Nia—' I begin but she stops looking at me. She is staring at Drew.

She takes a step backwards. Then another. She shakes her head, all the while taking steps away from me and away from the truth. 'No, that can't be true,' she says. 'No. No. It just can't be.'

'I'm so sorry, Nia,' I say.

Drew says nothing.

'No, no, no—' Nia turns and takes off up the slope from the beach to the resort, her sundress flapping in the breeze behind her as she runs.

Marvin is standing stock-still staring at his dad. His horror is clear on his face. He's waiting, I think, for his father to deny it. Drew is completely focused on his son but he doesn't say a word. Jake is staring at where Nia has just run off, clearly wondering if he should follow her.

Kwame and Edward look awkward and embarrassed. Working and living in a hotel, I'm sure they have heard all sorts of gossip over the years, but there'll be nothing like this. I can't worry about anyone else right now, though. I have to find my daughter.

Now

I expected to find Nia in her bedroom, crying or throwing up in the toilet. That is what I would be doing if I were her. Instead, she is in my bedroom. When I enter my room, she is tugging open a drawer from the dresser, reaching in and throwing everything in it on to the floor.

She does the same with the other four drawers in that chest – opening them, throwing things out, slamming them shut to get to the next one.

'What are you doing?' I ask her.

'Where is it?' she screeches as she opens my wardrobe and begins pulling out shoeboxes. She empties them and then throws them aside when she doesn't find whatever it is she's looking for.

'Where's what?' I ask.

'The picture of *him*. My father. I know you won't have got rid of it. I know it's here somewhere.'

Then she gets to the bedside table and opens those drawers – one, two, three. In number three she finds it. The furniture had come with us from Brighton and that is the place where I have always kept the picture of Drew. Waiting for the time when Nia would ask about him. I never could have imagined she would be looking for it in these circumstances. She takes out the photo of her father and me. It was very rare to get a photo of him, even rarer to have one of us together.

Nia looks at the photo for a few seconds, her eyes searching every inch to try to find something, anything, that will tell her he isn't related to her by blood. After she finds nothing to prove Drew isn't her father, she drops it. 'No, no, no,' she says. 'No.' She sinks to the floor and covers her face with her hands. 'No, no, no,' she keeps sobbing. 'No, no, no.'

I go to her, put my arms around her and hold her as she cries. 'I'm so sorry,' I say to her over and over. 'I'm so sorry.'

Jake arrives and is about to come in, but I hold my hand up and then wave him away. This isn't the place for him or anyone else. Right now, it needs to be just Nia and me.

Jake steps out of the room and shuts the door behind him. I take my daughter completely in my arms, then rock her back and forth, just like I did when she was a baby.

12

Now

'What on earth is going on?' Ellen, Marvin's mother, asks angrily when I wander out on to the patio outside the dining room.

The sun is coming up over the horizon and its heat on my skin is like a warm bath after a long trip to the Arctic. I have spent the night holding Nia while she sobbed. She couldn't speak, just cry. I hushed her, hugged her, tried to think of a way to make it right.

Now she is asleep and I need to move my body, to feel the sun on my skin to feel alive again. Part of the patio has a large corrugated roof, and part of it is exposed to the sun. Jake sits at the end that is exposed, staring at the sea and taking sips from a bottle of beer.

'I have just spent the whole night sitting with my sobbing son,' Ellen says, the anger still soaking her voice. I would be as angry as her if my child was in the state he was in, and I had no idea why. 'Marvin couldn't speak for crying, and every time I tried to leave him he started wailing. Actually wailing. I had to tuck him up in my bed and he's only just cried himself to sleep.

'On top of all that, I have no idea where Andrew is. Your staff refuse to answer any questions and keep offering me cups of tea. And your husband hasn't said a word in the half an hour I've been out here. What *is* going on?'

I drop into a chair facing the ocean, and throw my head back, trying to stretch my poor aching neck muscles.

'Has everyone around here taken leave of their senses?' Ellen asks.

'We need to find Drew,' I say. 'Once we do, we can sit down and talk about what to do next.'

'What to do next?' Ellen comes to stand in front of me. 'Has something happened with your daughter and my son?'

'We need to find Drew,' I repeat quietly. 'Then we can all talk.'

'Why do you say Andrew's name like that?' Ellen asks.

'Like what?'

'Like you've known him from before today. Nobody shortens his name – he doesn't like it. But you do it as if you've been given permission.'

I frown at her. Maybe she has blanked it out of her head. Twenty-four years is a long time. Maybe she has truly forgotten how she helped Drew leave here, how she had this place robbed. I suppose she had to have forgotten all about that to be able to come back here and act normally. 'When we find Drew, we can all sit down and talk,' I repeat.

'I'm right here,' he says from the doorway that leads into the dining room.

My stomach flips at his voice, at his arrival. Drew used to frighten me. I can admit that, now I know he is alive. I seemed to have forgotten that over the years of missing him. Over the years when he was dead to me, I tended to focus on remembering the good things about him. Every time something bad about his behaviour came up in my memory, I would shy away from it, bury it, pretend it wasn't as horrible as it was.

Yes, he was nice most of the time, and I loved him no matter what. But when it was bad, it was horrific. And it would have got worse. I can admit that now, too. I had put all those worries about his treatment of me to one side, especially when I found out I was pregnant and in the run-up to the wedding, because I didn't want to let anyone down. I wanted to believe that he would change once we were married and he'd become a dad. But he probably wouldn't have. Actually, he probably would have become more terrifying, once marriage and a baby had made it harder for me to leave him.

'Stay well away from me,' Jake warns from his place at the end of the patio, without looking around. 'Well away.'

'Where have you been?' Ellen asks Drew.

'Trying to clear my head,' he says to her. He definitely talks differently to her. He doesn't seem to be as confident and sure of himself with her. I can't imagine him ever screaming at her that he'd make her sorry if he ever caught her even looking at another man.

'Right, now we are all here, would someone mind telling me what is going on?' Ellen says as she takes a seat on the opposite side of the patio.

'It's all right, you can drop the act now,' I tell her. 'You can stop pretending.'

'Stop pretending about what exactly?' she says icily.

'Drew told me how you paid a couple of local boys to rob this place to get his passport back all those years ago.'

'I did what?' she says. She turns to her husband who is still standing by the doorway to the dining room. 'I did *what*?' she repeats, raising her voice.

'Tessa has got it mixed up,' Drew says quickly. 'Totally mixed up.'

'What about the part where Jake tried to kill you? Did I get that mixed up too?' I ask him.

'Is that what you told her?' Jake says, shaking his head without taking his eyes off the sea. 'You're creative, I'll give you that.'

'You, *shush*,' Ellen says to Jake. 'We are talking about me.' She looks at her husband again. 'I did *what*?'

Morning heat is my favourite type of warmth. It feels like someone is turning on the sun like they would an oven, getting it ready to do everything it needs to that day. I close my eyes, heavy and gritty as they are, lift my face to the sun, and wait for Drew to speak.

Of course he doesn't. Coward that he is.

'I need someone to start at the beginning and tell me exactly what is going on,' Ellen eventually says. 'I will not be held responsible if someone doesn't start talking.'

'Twenty-four years ago,' I say, 'I was meant to get married on the beach here. During the wedding, a little boy was washed out to sea and my husband-to-be, his best man and a couple of members of staff ran into the water to rescue him. The boy was saved, but my husband-to-be was killed.'

'Oh my, that is awful. I'm so sorry,' she says. 'But what has this got to do with anything, particularly why I have been up all night with my crying son?'

'I was meant to be marrying Drew. Sorry, Andrew.'

Ellen's eyes widen in shock. 'How can that be? *I* met him twenty-four years ago,' she says. 'First of all at that quaint little village market, and then he came to visit me at my hotel. A couple of days after that, he moved hotels and checked in at the same place where I was staying. He said he couldn't stand to be away from me.'

'And you were the most beautiful woman he had ever met – your destiny was shaped by the stars?' I ask.

'He said all those things to you too?' Ellen replies.

I nod.

'You're making it sound calculated,' Drew says. 'It wasn't like that. Not at all. I loved you.' He looks at me when he says this. 'I love you.' He looks at Ellen when he says that. 'Those words are the only way I can express myself.'

'Are we supposed to forget that you faked your own death to get out of marrying Tessa?' Jake adds. 'Or that, apparently, I tried to kill you?'

'And I don't understand about me paying

someone to break into this place?' Ellen adds. 'The first time I heard of Bussu Bay was when Marvin said he was getting married here. I told him and Nia that I had been to Ghana once. That I'd met Andrew there. But I'd never heard of this place. I was surprised how close it was to that hotel I stayed in.'

'You mean, when Drew managed to survive Jake's murder attempt at sea, you didn't take him in at your hotel and let him hide out in your room? And you didn't then plot to get his passport back by paying a couple of local boys to turn over the place?' I say. I knew it was nonsense, but Drew always had a way of planting that little seed of doubt in my mind.

'I wouldn't even know where to start with something like that!' Ellen replies. 'I was here on a modelling assignment. I met Andrew the one morning I ventured out to the market. The rest of the time I spent at the hotel. So shoot me, I like being near a pool, I like my drinks served cold and I like reclining on a sun lounger.

'Drew joined me at the hotel after a couple of days. Although, thinking about it now, I do remember him saying he'd left his passport behind so he had to go back to his original hotel. I did think it odd that he had a bonfire on the beach a couple of nights later. And he borrowed money to change his plane ticket, so he could get the same flight home as me.'

Oh my God. '*You* broke in here, didn't you?' I say to Drew. '*You* stole all our ID and you burned it. You trapped us here. You made our nightmare worse, just so you could get close to Ellen.'

'It took weeks to sort that mess out,' Jake says. 'New passports and tickets and cancelling cards. You did that to us? Just so you could go off with another woman.'

'It wasn't like that,' Drew insists. 'I felt trapped. It was all happening so fast. I was so young and I was being forced to get married.'

'Drew, I didn't want to get married. It was all you talked about, right from when we met. You gave me that terrible choice – either we got married and had a baby, or you would leave me. I was so in love with you back then that I went along with it. I didn't want any of it.'

'He told me that you were threatening to dump him if he didn't marry you,' Jake states. 'That was why I stepped aside – you wanted to marry him.'

'He told me that he'd never wanted to marry anyone before,' Ellen tells us. 'We married within two months of getting home.'

'Because I love you,' Drew protests.

'I seriously doubt that,' Jake says. 'I'm guessing Ellen's family are rich? Like you thought Tessa's family were rich because they'd built a hotel?'

'What?' Ellen and I ask at the same time.

'You like money, don't you, Drew?' Jake says. 'You especially like women with money or access to family money.'

'You know nothing about me,' Drew tells Jake.

Jake laughs. 'What's to know? You're a liar. My guess is that when Nia and Marvin said where they were getting married and that her mum owned the place, you realised Nia was Tessa's daughter. You couldn't get out of coming to the wedding, so you came up with some story about me trying to kill you. Hoping that would convince Tessa to keep it quiet to protect you both.'

'You know nothing about it,' Drew spits.

'It's so obvious: you met Ellen and realised she was from money, and decided to get out of marrying Tessa. What was the original plan, eh, Drew? Disappear into the bush one night, never to be heard from again? You must have been over the moon when that boy ended up in the sea and it gave you a chance to disappear. I bet you didn't even try to save him; you just went off in that direction and then headed off when we were all distracted.'

'Shut up,' Drew replies.

'What I don't get is how you thought you'd get away with it now we're all together here?' Jake says. 'Did you really think you'd be able to keep us all apart? Didn't you think we'd talk about it? This is all so Drew. You think the world will let you get away with anything and everything. And it does for a while. But not for ever. Never for ever.'

'Just shut up,' Drew repeats.

Ellen, who has been silent, cuts in: 'What has any of this got to do with why my son is so upset? I mean, it's all shocking and everything for everyone here, but the important person in all of this is my son. Why is Marvin so distraught?'

'I was pregnant when I was meant to be getting married,' I say to her. She can join up the dots from there.

'So what? I was pregnant too, when I . . .' Her voice trails away when the realisation hits her. 'Nia is your daughter?' Ellen asks Drew.

He does not reply; he simply continues to lean against the doorway.

'Yes, Nia is his daughter. Which means . . .'

'Does Marvin know this?' Ellen demands. 'Is this why he was so distressed?' She stands up. 'My poor baby. I must go to him.'

Drew points a finger at Ellen, then jabs it towards her chair. 'Sit down. No one's going anywhere until we work out how we're going to manage this mess.'

'I'm going to my son – he needs me,' Ellen replies.

'Ellen, so help me, I'll—'

'You'll what, Andrew?' she says, turning on him. 'You'll stop living off my father's money? You'll go out into the real world, and try to find another job where everyone around you has to keep correcting your mistakes without complaining because you're married to the boss's daughter? You'll give up your nice little sports car? You'll move out of our house and spend years fighting me in court for access to my money? What will you do exactly, Andrew?'

He says nothing now that she has shown him quite clearly how much she rules things. That is why he speaks to her differently – she is in control of their relationship. She is in control because she can take away his luxury lifestyle whenever she wants and he knows that. 'Andrew, my son will always come before anyone on this Earth, including you.'

Drew lowers his head for a moment.

'And, please note, I said "*my*" son. Have you never noticed that I always say "*my* son"?'

'What does that mean?' Drew asks.

'I was pregnant when we met.'

Drew shakes his head. 'No you weren't.'

'Yes, I was. I was in that market that day to find some ginger to help with morning sickness. One of the maids at the hotel told me it would help because I seemed to develop it from day one. I was having an affair with the photographer from the shoot. But he was married and wanted nothing to do with me. Then you showed up. You were my type, and I knew you would never be able to tell the difference. You weren't interested in anything other than getting away from Ghana. And, after that, you weren't interested in anything but my family's money. Which was perfect for me, really, because I could do whatever I wanted without any interference from you.'

My heart leaps in my chest. It's OK. Nia and Marvin aren't related. They aren't brother and sister.

'It's not true,' Drew says.

'Oh yes it is,' Ellen replies. 'Marvin is not your son. Which means he is not Nia's brother. Which means they can get married as planned.'

'Oh thank you!' I cry, jumping to my feet. 'I have to tell Nia. Thank you so much!'

'My pleasure,' she replies. 'Oh, and Andrew, you had better find somewhere else to sleep. I do not want to see your face again for the next few days.'

13

Now

I have tucked up Nia and Marvin in the Honeymoon Suite, so they can get a full day's sleep to make up for last night. The moment they were both told the good news Marvin came flying into the main part of the resort and they almost leapt into each other's arms outside my bedroom.

Ellen and I watched our children sobbing and holding each other like they'd never let the other one go ever again. I knew Marvin would have a lot of questions for his mother about his biological father, but, at that moment, nothing else mattered to him or Nia.

I wanted to ask Ellen what she would do next – whether she would stay with Drew, or if things were over for them – but I held my tongue. Whatever Ellen did next, I had a feeling she was going to be perfectly fine.

I have given the staff the rest of the day off, and I have no idea where Drew has gone. I climb into bed, waiting for Jake to appear. When he doesn't after an hour or so, I go to find him. He's sitting in the same place where he sat earlier. He doesn't look like he's moved all night or morning.

'I think we should all just write off today and start again tomorrow,' I say to him. 'Are you coming to bed?'

'Do you want me to?' He doesn't look at me as he speaks, simply continues to stare at the ocean.

'Of course I do,' I reply.

'I don't think that's true. I don't think you've ever really wanted me, and something Drew told you gave you the perfect excuse to shut me out.'

I cover my face with my hands for a few seconds. 'It wasn't so much what he said. It was just ... I didn't understand why you started fighting him straight away, that's all. He was your best friend and you didn't seem relieved he was alive; you were just angry and you attacked him.'

'I *was* relieved. When you told me on the phone I was very relieved and happy, but on the drive back I had time to think. And I realised this was typical Drew. He was my best mate, but he's a spineless coward. Always has been. He would always go for the easiest route, would avoid anything that meant hard work or facing up to his actions.

'He has put us through hell for more than twenty years, and Nia has grown up without a father all because he was too much of a coward to just finish with you. Because that was what this was all about. He found someone he thought was better, but couldn't dump you in a normal way. No, he has to go through all that crap at the wedding. By the time I got here I was so angry I couldn't control myself.'

'But that's just it, Jake, you are one of the kindest, most gentle men I know – except where Drew is involved. When it's about Drew, you're telling me you fought him over me, you tell me you'll kill him if he hurts me. That's a part of you I don't understand. You're not violent. You're not crazy. And you're not even particularly jealous, until it comes to Drew and me. Drew told me you were obsessive. That you've been obsessive about other women in the past. It scared me, to be honest.'

'I'm not obsessive. But I just couldn't stand the thought of him treating you like he treated his other girlfriends. Not when I loved you so much.'

'But you didn't know me.'

'I know, but in twenty-odd years, I haven't stopped loving you, have I?'

'True.'

'And Drew knew that you were special because . . . Tessa, you're the only woman I've been with.'

'What? That's not true. You had girlfriends before me.'

'I did, but I never went beyond a few kisses with any of them. I always wanted to wait until I got married before I lost my virginity. I know most men aren't like that, but it was important to me. Always had been. Then I met you and I . . . I changed my mind. Stupidly, I told Drew all about you. He knew how I felt about you, but he'd also heard all about your parents building a hotel and he thought you came from money, so he went for you. Which is why I wasn't going to let him hurt you. If I'd kept my mouth shut, hadn't told him about your parents' hotel, he probably wouldn't have targeted you in the way he did.'

'So you don't think he ever loved me?'

'As much as someone like him can fall in love, yeah, I think he did. You certainly loved him.'

'And I loved you, as well.' There, said it. Said it, mean it.

Jake stares at me warily.

'I love you,' I repeat. 'And you were wrong – Nia did have a father growing up. You. You are, and always have been, the best father for her.'

'Thank you,' he says quietly.

'And I was wondering,' I begin. 'I was wondering if . . . if you would marry me in a few days' time? Down on the beach, around about the time our daughter does it?'

He blinks at me. 'Are you sure?' he replies.

'Yes,' I say. 'Absolutely sure.'

14

Now

'And he didn't even ask her,' my mother says to my father as I walk past her down our makeshift aisle. 'She had to ask him. What kind of nonsense is that?'

I grin at my mother's outrage that I am finally doing what she wanted me to do, but it's still not right. Jake and I drove up to Accra to tell them about Drew – they were both horrified at first, then relieved. Then angry and so, so hurt. None of us can really understand why he did it, but my dad's final words on the subject were: 'If I see him, I will set the dogs on him.'

Nia beams at me when I arrive to stand next to her. Jake is beside me and Marvin beside Nia. The wedding has been delayed a couple of days so Jake's friends and family from England and the Bahamas could fly over to watch us get married. It's going to be an incredible party.

While the congregation finishes the first hymn, Nia leans towards me and whispers: 'This is the best present you could ever have given me, Mum. It's what I've wanted for the longest time.'

'I know,' I reply.

'Thank you,' she says. 'Now all you have to do is work out how to get me a brother or sister.'

THE END

Acknowledgements

I'm so grateful to the many people that have helped to make this Quick Reads stories happen.

Thank you to:

the people at my publishers including but not only: Susan, Viola and Cass;

my lovely agents: Ant and James;

the team at Quick Reads & the Reading Agency, including but not only: Fanny, Louise and David;

you, the reader. Thank you for buying this book and supporting literacy.

About Quick Reads

Quick Reads are brilliant short new books written by bestselling writers. They are perfect for regular readers wanting a fast and satisfying read, but they are also ideal for adults who are discovering reading for pleasure for the first time.

Since Quick Reads was founded In 2006, over 4.5 million copies of more than a hundred titles have been sold or distributed. Quick Reads are available in paperback, in ebook and from your local library.

To find out more about Quick Reads titles, visit
www.readingagency.org.uk/quickreads

Quick Reads is part of The Reading Agency,
the leading charity inspiring people of all ages and all backgrounds to read for pleasure and empowerment. Working with our partners, our aim is to make reading accessible to everyone. The Reading Agency is funded by the Arts Council.

www.readingagency.org.uk Tweet us @readingagency

The Reading Agency Ltd • Registered number: 3904882 (England & Wales) Registered charity number: 1085443 (England & Wales) Registered Office: Free Word Centre, 60 Farringdon Road, London, EC1R 3GA The Reading Agency is supported using public funding by Arts Council England.

We would like to thank all our funders and a range of private donors who believe in the value of our work.

LOTTERY FUNDED

ARTS COUNCIL ENGLAND

THE
READING
AGENCY

has something for everyone

Stories to make you laugh

Stories to make you feel good

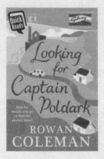

Stories to take you to another place

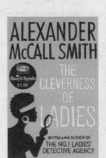

Stories about real life

Stories to take you to another time

Stories to make you turn the pages

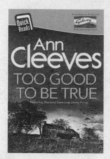

For a complete list of titles visit

www.readingagency.org.uk/quickreads

Available in paperback, ebook and from your local library

Why not start a reading group?

If you have enjoyed this book, why not share your next Quick Read with friends, colleagues, or neighbours?

The Reading Agency also runs **Reading Groups for Everyone** which helps you discover and share new books. Find a reading group near you, or register a group you already belong to and get free books and offers from publishers at **readinggroups.org**

There is a free toolkit with lots of ideas to help you run a Quick Reads reading group at **www.readingagency.org.uk/quickreads**

Share your experiences of your group on Twitter

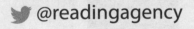 @readingagency

Continuing your reading journey

As well as Quick Reads, The Reading Agency runs lots of programmes to help keep you and your family reading.

Reading Ahead invites you to pick six reads and record your reading in a diary to get a certificate **readingahead.org.uk**

World Book Night is an annual celebration of reading and books on 23 April **worldbooknight.org**

Chatterbooks children's reading groups and the **Summer Reading Challenge** inspire children to read more and share the books they love **readingagency.org.uk/children**

ALSO FROM DOROTHY KOOMSON...

'Do you ever wonder if you've lived the life you were meant to?' I ask her. She sighs, and dips her head. 'Even if I do, what difference will it make?'

In 1988, two eight-year-old girls with almost identical names and the same love of ballet meet for the first time. They seem destined to be best friends forever and to become professional dancers.

Years later, however, they have both been dealt so many cruel blows that they walk away from each other into very different futures – one enters a convent, the other becomes a minor celebrity. Will these new, 'invisible' lives be the ones they were meant to live, or will they only find that kind of salvation when they are reunited twenty years later?

arrow books

ALSO FROM DOROTHY KOOMSON...

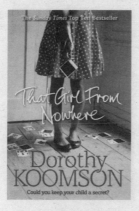

'Where are you coming from with that accent of yours?'
he asks. 'Nowhere,' I reply. 'I'm from nowhere.' 'Everyone's
from somewhere,' he says. 'Not me,' I reply silently.

Clemency Smittson was adopted as a baby and the
only connection she has to her birth mother is a cardboard
box hand-decorated with butterflies. Now an adult, Clem
decides to make a drastic life change and move to Brighton,
where she was born. Clem has no idea that while there
she'll meet someone who knows all about her butterfly box
and what happened to her birth parents.

As the tangled truths about her adoption and childhood start
to unravel, a series of shocking events cause Clem to reassess
whether the price of having contact with her birth family could
be too high to pay . . .

arrow books

What secrets would you kill to keep?

After her husband's big promotion, Cece Solarin arrives
in Brighton with their three children, ready to start afresh.
But their new neighbourhood has a deadly secret.

Three weeks earlier, Yvonne, a very popular parent, was almost
murdered in the grounds of the local school – the same school
where Cece has unwittingly enrolled her children.

Already anxious about making friends when the parents
seem so cliquey, Cece is now also worried about her children's
safety. By chance she meets Maxie, Anaya and Hazel,
three very different school mothers who make her feel
welcome and reassure her about her new life.

That is until Cece discovers the police believe one of her new
friends tried to kill Yvonne. Reluctant to spy on her friends but
determined to discover the truth, Cece must uncover the poten-
tial murderer before they strike again . . .

a r r o w   b o o k s